Clifford's
Good Deeds

Story and pictures by NORMAN BRIDWELL

FOUR WINDS PRESS   NEW YORK

PUBLISHED BY FOUR WINDS PRESS

A DIVISION OF SCHOLASTIC MAGAZINES, INC., NEW YORK, N.Y.

COPYRIGHT © 1975 BY NORMAN BRIDWELL

PRINTED IN THE UNITED STATES OF AMERICA

LIBRARY OF CONGRESS CATALOG CARD NUMBER: 75–15463

ISBN 0–590–07439–3

1 2 3 4 5   80 79 78 77 76

For Tim, Steve, and Paul

Hello. I'm Emily Elizabeth.
This is my dog, Clifford.

A boy named Tim lives across the street.

One day Tim said, "I try to do
a good deed every day. If I had Clifford
I could help a lot of people."

I said, "Let's do some good deeds together."

A man was raking leaves. We wanted
to help him put the leaves in his truck.

I didn't know that dry leaves...

...make Clifford sneeze.

The man said he didn't need any more help.
We went down the street.

We saw a lady painting her fence.

We helped her paint.
When we finished she thanked us.

Clifford felt so happy that he wagged his tail.
That was a mistake.

We said we would paint her house too.
The lady said, "Never mind."

Then we saw an old lady
trying to get her kitten down from a tree.
Tim said, "Clifford, get the kitty."

Clifford bent the limb down
so the lady could reach her kitten.

But his paw slipped.

Clifford moves pretty fast for a big dog.

The lady was glad to get her kitten back.

It didn't take us long to find
our next good deed to do.

Somebody had let the air out of the tires
of a car. The man asked if we could help him.

Tim took a rubber tube out of the car
and stuck it on the tire valve. Then
he told Clifford to blow air through the tube.

Clifford blew.

But he blew a little too hard.

The man felt better
when we took his car to a garage.

We saw a small paperboy.
He was so small that he couldn't throw
the newspapers to the doorsteps.

Clifford gave him a hand. I mean a paw.

Clifford was a little too strong.

Nothing seemed to go right for us.
All our good deeds were turning out wrong.

Then we saw a terrible thing. A man was hurt and lying in the street. Nobody was helping him.

Tim said, "You should never move
an injured person." Clifford didn't hear him.
He picked the man up.

We started off to find a doctor. Oh dear.

We helped the men get their cable back down the manhole. Tim said, "Clifford, maybe you shouldn't help me any more."

Clifford felt very sad. He had tried so hard to do the right things. We headed for home.

Suddenly we heard somebody shouting, "Help! Fire!"

The house on the corner was on fire.
Tim ran to the alarm box
to call the fire department.

Clifford ran to the burning house.
There were two little kids upstairs.

With Clifford's help...

...we got them out safely.

Luckily, there was a swimming pool in the yard.

Clifford put out the fire
just as the firemen were arriving.

The firemen finished the job
and thanked us for our help.

That afternoon the mayor gave us each
a medal for our good deeds.

Of course, Clifford got the biggest medal of all.

More books about Clifford by Norman Bridwell

All of these books are available in paperback editions from Scholastic Book Services.

Clifford, the Big Red Dog*

Clifford Gets a Job

Clifford Takes a Trip

Clifford's Halloween*

Clifford's Tricks

Clifford, the Small Red Puppy

Clifford's Riddles

*Also available in hardcover from Four Winds Press